Henry's 100 Days of Kindergarten

by Nancy Carlson

VIKING

For Mikey,
the only kindergartner in history who
jumped out the window on his first day of school.
Luckily your room was on the first floor!!!
Love, Mom

VIKING
Published by Penguin Group
Penguin Young Readers Group, 345 Hudson Street, New York, New York 10014, U.S.A.
Penguin Group (Canada), 10 Alcorn Avenue, Toronto, Ontario, Canada M4V 3B2
(a division of Pearson Penguin Canada Inc.)
Penguin Books Ltd, 80 Strand, London WC2R 0RL, England
Penguin Ireland, 25 St Stephen's Green, Dublin 2, Ireland (a division of Penguin Books Ltd)
Penguin Group (Australia), 250 Camberwell Road, Camberwell, Victoria 3124, Australia
(a division of Pearson Australia Group Pty Ltd)
Penguin Books India Pvt Ltd, 11 Community Centre, Panchsheel Park, New Delhi - 110 017, India
Penguin Group (NZ), Cnr Airborne and Rosedale Roads, Albany, Auckland, New Zealand
(a division of Pearson New Zealand Ltd)
Penguin Books (South Africa) (Pty) Ltd, 24 Sturdee Avenue, Rosebank, Johannesburg 2196, South Africa

Penguin Books Ltd, Registered Offices: 80 Strand, London WC2R 0RL, England

Published in 2004 by Viking, a division of Penguin Young Readers Group.

1 3 5 7 9 10 8 6 4 2

LIBRARY OF CONGRESS CATALOGING-IN-PUBLICATION DATA
Carlson, Nancy L.
Henry's 100 days of kindergarten / by Nancy Carlson.
p.   cm.
Summary: To celebrate the one hundredth day of kindergarten, each student brings in an example of 100 for show-and-tell,
including a 100-year-old relative, and Ms. Bradley shares the jar of 100 jelly beans that have marked the days.
ISBN 0-670-05977-3 (hardcover)
[1. Hundredth Day of School—Fiction. 2. Kindergarten—Fiction. 3. Hundred (The number)—Fiction. 4. Schools—Fiction.
5. Show-and-tell presentations—Fiction.] I. Title: Henry's one hundred days of kindergarten. II. Title.
PZ7.C21665Hd 2004
[E]—dc22
2004004531

Manufactured in China
Set in Avenir
Book designed by Kelley McIntyre

# SEPTEMBER

In September, on the very first day of kindergarten, Ms. Bradley said, "Each day of school I will add a jelly bean to this jar.

"When there are 100 jelly beans in the jar, we'll have a party to celebrate 100 days of kindergarten," said Ms. Bradley. "Everyone can bring in 100 things to share for show and tell *and* we can eat all the jelly beans!"
"Yummy!" said Henry.

"But for now we've got pictures to color, songs to learn, and letters to print!"

OCTOBER

In October, Henry learned it's not a good idea to bring a pet spider for show and tell,

especially when it gets lost in the classroom.

On Halloween, all the kindergartners dressed up

in their costumes for a Halloween parade.

NOVEMBER

In November, Henry and his classmates shared a big Thanksgiving feast.

Then all the kindergartners showed pictures of
what they were thankful for.

DECEMBER

One day in December, Henry and his classmates
were so excited when it started to snow

that Ms. Bradley decided they should all
play outside!

Just before the winter break,

the kindergartners put on a holiday concert.

JANUARY

In January, when the class went to the school library, Henry discovered a very favorite book.

Henry had his father, his mother, and even the babysitter read him the book over and over, until he had it memorized.

FEBRUARY

Finally in February, it was the 100th day of kindergarten. When Ms. Bradley put the 100th jelly bean in the jar, the class cheered.

Then it was time to show their 100 things. Suzy had made a paper-clip chain with 100 paper clips.

Parker showed 100 words he knew.

Tony showed a house he had built made of 100 Popsicle sticks.

100 MarSHMallows

Sydney had only 98 marshmallows glued on cardboard, because she ate two on the way to school!

When it was Henry's turn Ms. Bradley said, "No spiders I hope."
"Nope . . . but I would like to introduce you to . . . bring her in, Mom!"

"This is my great-grandma Millie.
She is 100 years old!"

"Wow, she's even older than you, Ms. Bradley," said Tony.

The kindergartners had lots of questions

Then Ms. Bradley said, "Now it's time for jelly beans, and everyone gets . . .

five!"
"Hey, that's not very many," said Tony.
"Why do we only get five?" asked Henry.

So Ms. Bradley made a chart showing that 100 jelly beans divided by 20 kindergartners equals 5 jelly beans each.

"But five jelly beans isn't much of a party.
That's why I made . . .

a cake with 100 candles!"
"Wow! That's a lot of candles!" said Henry.

As everyone enjoyed the cake, Henry said, "I sure hope there's another 100 days of kindergarten . . .

because kindergarten is so much fun!"
"It sure is!" said Great-Grandma Millie.